GREEN LANTERN

Hal Jordan:
Defender of Earth

adapted by Jake Black
illustrated by Steven E. Gordon

screenplay by Greg Berlanti & Michael Green &
Marc Guggenheim and Michael Goldberg, screenstory by Greg
Berlanti & Michael Green & Marc Guggenheim, based upon
characters appearing in comic books published by DC Comics.

PSS!
PRICE STERN SLOAN
An Imprint of Penguin Group (USA) Inc.

PRICE STERN SLOAN
Published by the Penguin Group
Penguin Group (USA) Inc., 375 Hudson Street, New York, New York 10014, USA
Penguin Group (Canada), 90 Eglinton Avenue East, Suite 700, Toronto, Ontario M4P 2Y3, Canada (a division of Pearson Penguin Canada Inc.)
Penguin Books Ltd., 80 Strand, London WC2R 0RL, England
Penguin Group Ireland, 25 St. Stephen's Green, Dublin 2, Ireland (a division of Penguin Books Ltd.)
Penguin Group (Australia), 250 Camberwell Road, Camberwell, Victoria 3124, Australia (a division of Pearson Australia Group Pty. Ltd.)
Penguin Books India Pvt. Ltd., 11 Community Centre, Panchsheel Park, New Delhi—110 017, India
Penguin Group (NZ), 67 Apollo Drive, Rosedale, Auckland 0632, New Zealand (a division of Pearson New Zealand Ltd.)
Penguin Books (South Africa) (Pty.) Ltd., 24 Sturdee Avenue, Rosebank, Johannesburg 2196, South Africa
Penguin Books Ltd., Registered Offices: 80 Strand, London WC2R 0RL, England

ISBN 978-0-8431-9841-6   10 9 8 7 6 5 4 3 2 1

Coast City was one of the best places in the world. It had beautiful beaches, stunning landscapes, and friendly neighborhoods. It was also home to Ferris Aircraft. Ferris was known for building some of the best military aircraft in the world. To eleven-year-old Hal Jordan, between Coast City and Ferris Aircraft, there was no better place to be a kid. He loved living in Coast City and learning everything there was to know about Ferris's planes.

Hal spent a lot of time playing at Ferris Aircraft. His dad, Martin Jordan, was a test pilot, so Hal was always at the airplane hangars. He was good friends with one of the other kids at Ferris, too: Carol Ferris, the daughter of the company's founder. Hal and Carol were often seen together watching their dads reveal the newest airplanes. They were best friends.

One morning, Hal and his dad went to Ferris for another airplane demonstration. Martin prepared for the test flight, and Hal met up with Carol. Carol was happy to see her friend, and even had a small crush on him. Hal liked being with Carol, too, even though he didn't realize her crush. All he really cared about was watching his dad soar through the air. Hal believed his dad was the best test pilot in the world.

Hal knew his dad was completely fearless. He longed to be just like his dad, but knew deep down that would be hard. Hal was scared of a lot of things. Still, today he was prouder than he'd ever been of his father. Hal cheered as he saw his dad's plane take off into the sky. It was another big accomplishment for Martin personally, and for Ferris Aircraft as a whole. It was a new era in flight.

As Martin's plane soared skyward, Hal grinned from ear to ear. But his excitement didn't last long. The plane started acting funny; it was making strange noises. A moment later, Hal watched his father's plane burst into flames and explode in a giant fireball. Martin was gone. Hal had lost his father—his hero. He knew that he would never be the same again. He loved his dad more than anything in the world and now his dad was gone. Hal was crushed.

Fifteen years later, and millions of miles above Earth, in the darkness of deep space, a strange alien spaceship sped through the stars. It was a huge ship on its way toward a rescue mission. In the pilot's seat sat a magenta-skinned alien named Abin Sur. He wore a green uniform and a glowing ring on his finger. He was very focused on what he had to do to complete his mission. His fingers danced across the ship's controls, increasing its speed.

Abin Sur's glowing ring flickered, and a holographic image of another Green Lantern, Sinestro, appeared.

"Sinestro, I am traveling at maximum velocity," Abin Sur said. "Tell Fentara I should reach his sector by——"

"Your rescue mission to that planet is no longer necessary. It has been destroyed," Sinestro interrupted, speaking ominously. "It is just as it was on Talok, every life-form gone."

Abin Sur was saddened by the tragic news Sinestro had given him.

"What are the Guardians' orders?" Abin asked.

"The Guardians are silent," Sinestro said.

Abin grew worried. If so many lives in the universe were at risk, why were the Guardians not giving orders to better protect the planets and their people? Something was wrong. Since the beginning of time, the Guardians had protected the universe. Why stop now? It made no sense. Still Abin remained a loyal warrior for the Guardians.

Suddenly, Abin Sur's spaceship rocked violently, sending the pilot to the ground. Sinestro's image flickered and faded from the ring. The ship continued rocking and shaking. It was under attack by an unknown force or object. Abin tried to see what it was, but couldn't. The ship's sensors were down. Whatever it was, it was tearing the ship apart. A large chunk of the damaged vessel swung at Abin, severely injuring him. He staggered away from the controls.

Abin was in pain, but was able to pull himself into an escape pod on the side of the ship. With great effort, he closed the pod's door and blasted away from the main ship. He watched through the window as the ship exploded in an amazing fireball. Abin had been fortunate to get away from his vessel before it was destroyed, but the escape had come at a great cost. He had been mortally wounded.

As his escape pod drifted away from the ship's debris, Abin ordered the pod's computer to find the nearest life-sustaining planet. The computer located a blue sphere covered by water and land: Earth. Abin rested, trying to recover from his injuries, while the pod made its way toward Earth. Abin knew Earth was a primitive planet. Its people had never seen alien life before. He had no idea how humans would react to him.

Fifteen years after his dad's tragic accident, Hal Jordan became a test pilot himself for Ferris Aircraft. He worked very hard to become the best test pilot at Ferris. As he reached the top, though, he stopped working hard. Flying came naturally to him, but he didn't take it very seriously. His attitude annoyed the people he worked with. Even Carol had grown frustrated with Hal. Hal had become irresponsible, lazy, and unreliable.

On a bright, sunny day, much like the one on which Hal watched his father crash, Carol Ferris and her family's company unveiled new fighter planes that didn't need pilots. These automated planes, called Sabres, were designed by Martin to prevent the deaths of pilots. Hal was assigned to fly a traditional plane in an exhibition against the automated aircraft. As the time for the exhibition drew close, Hal was nowhere to be seen.

As usual, Hal had overslept and arrived late to the demonstration. Carol was annoyed.

"I used to sleep in, too, Hal, but not since I was eleven!" she exclaimed.

Hal shrugged it off. He was the best pilot at Ferris, and they needed him to show off the new technology.

Carol continued, hoping Hal would listen this time. "I've gone up against the Sabres all week. There's nothing you can do that they can't do better or faster."

Hal ignored Carol's warning. He believed humans would always make better pilots than automated computers, no matter how fast or efficient they seemed. He strode away from Carol, confident that he would prove his belief. Hal jumped into the cockpit of his plane and took off. Two Sabres also headed for the skies. Carol had arranged a mock battle to show off the Sabres' abilities. Hal was excited to show off what he could do, too.

The mock battle began. Hal was ordered to fire his weapons at the Sabres. The Sabres elegantly weaved through the sky, avoiding Hal's blasts. The Sabres fired back at Hal, nearly hitting him. The Sabres were good. Hal had to prove that humans were better. Somehow he had to destroy the Sabres and live to tell about it. He knew Carol would be mad, but he had to show he was right.

Hal used his expertise as a pilot to confuse the automated planes. He flew his plane high into the atmosphere. The automated planes followed. The Sabres didn't realize the danger in flying so high. They only followed their orders. The Sabres soared higher and began to break apart. Hal's plane broke apart as well. He ejected himself from his plane as it blew up. Seconds later, the Sabres also exploded. Hal had won.

On the ground below, Carol and the other Ferris workers were mad at Hal. By showing that humans were better pilots, Hal may have cost Ferris several government contracts. Many people would lose their jobs.

"What were you doing, Hal?!" Carol angrily yelled.

"I thought the objective was to win," Hal said sarcastically.

"The objective was to show what the Sabres can do," Carol said through gritted teeth.

"I showed what they can't do," Hal said. "Winning takes more than cold computer logic."

Carol's father, Carl, stepped between Hal and Carol. He was just as angry as Carol.

"That's enough, Carol," Carl said. "Hal, I'm going to have to lay off most of my staff, and it's your fault."

Hal tried not to care, but he knew that he'd made a bad decision. He knew that if his father were alive, he'd be disappointed in him. Hal stormed out of Ferris Aircraft, angry at Carol and Carl, but even angrier at himself.

Not far from the Ferris Aircraft testing airfield, high in the atmosphere, a small alien spacecraft cut through the sky. Abin Sur's escape pod had arrived on Earth. Moving at speeds much faster than the speed of sound, the ship plummeted toward the ground below. Abin Sur tried piloting the tiny vessel, but couldn't because of his wounds. The escape pod crashed down in a massive explosion. Abin Sur slowly crawled out of the wreckage.

The crash made Abin Sur's injuries worse than they'd been before. He was dying. He could feel it. He knew that he had something very important to do before life left him. He extended his hand in front of him.

With his little remaining strength, he whispered, "Choose well."

The green ring on Abin's finger burst to life. It flew off his hand and quickly out into the unknown region beyond the crash site.

Later that night, Hal attended his nephew Jason's birthday party. Jason's parents were disappointed in Hal for being so reckless in the demonstration. But Hal didn't care. He went into Jason's bedroom to talk to his nephew.

"Were you scared, Uncle Hal?" Jason asked.

"No. I'm never scared," Hal lied. He had been very scared.

Jason believed Hal and left the room. Hal stayed sitting on Jason's bed, thinking about how scared he'd actually been. Suddenly the whole room started to shake. An eerie green glow filled the room. Hal looked around. He was a little scared. He didn't know what was happening. Was it an earthquake? The green light grew brighter and brighter. And then, as quickly as it started, the room stopped shaking and the light faded. Hal Jordan was gone.

Hal found himself by a lake near a crashed aircraft. He saw a body near the wreckage and moved to help. He was shocked to see that it was an alien. Abin Sur looked up at Hal and opened his hand. There was a green ring sitting on his magenta palm.

"The ring . . . chose . . . you . . . ," Abin said with great difficulty. "Lantern . . . "

The ring flew toward Hal.

"Great honor . . . responsibility . . . ," Abin struggled to say.

Abin Sur breathed his final breath and closed his eyes. The green uniform he'd been wearing faded into his magenta skin. He was gone. Hal took the ring and, still confused about what had just happened, put it on his finger. Green energy, like the light in Jason's room, surrounded Hal. He shielded his eyes, protecting them from the green brightness. Hal knew from that moment, his life would never be the same.

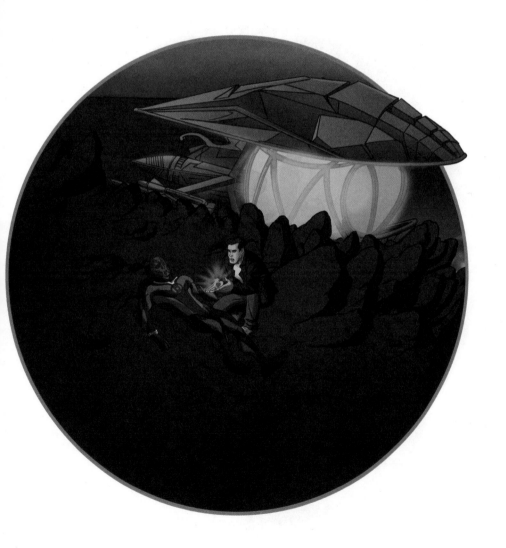

Hal returned to his apartment and stared at the ring. He still didn't understand what it all meant. The alien had said, "Lantern," and Hal had seen an object that looked like a lantern at the crash site. He had taken the Lantern with him. He pointed the ring at the Lantern and instinctively said, "In brightest day, in blackest night, no evil shall escape my sight. Let those who worship evil's might beware my power . . . Green Lantern's Light!"

Green energy burst from the Lantern, surging around Hal. In a flash he was transported to a distant alien planet—Oa. Hal looked around, examining his new surroundings. He was dressed in a uniform just like Abin Sur's. The lantern symbol on Hal's uniform shone brightly. He determined this must have been the alien's home planet.

"A human. This must mean Abin Sur is gone," a voice said behind Hal. Hal turned to see a fishlike alien approaching him. "Welcome to Oa."

The alien moved closer to Hal.

"A talking fish?" Hal said.

"I am Tomar-Re," the alien said. "A Green Lantern."

Hal stared in amazement at Tomar-Re. This was a lot of new information to take in.

"You are the first human to ever be chosen to wear the ring," Tomar-Re said. "An interesting choice for sure. The ring has never chosen a member of such a young species."

"What is all this?" Hal asked.

Tomar-Re motioned to the area around them. "Oa has been our home for countless millennia. It was created by the Guardians," he said. "The Guardians are immortal, responsible for all we are, all we do."

Hal raised his eyebrows, asking "Which is?"

"We are the Green Lantern Corps. We are the keepers of peace, justice, and order throughout the universe," Tomar-Re said. "Fly with me, human."

"Flying I can do," Hal said confidently as he and Tomar-Re floated into the air.

Hal and Tomar-Re flew toward the Great Hall. Together they entered the gigantic building. An enormous Lantern stood in the middle of the hall.

"That is the Central Power Battery, from which all Green Lantern power comes," Tomar-Re explained. "It gets its power from the will of every creature. It charges your Lantern, which in turn charges your ring."

Surrounding the Battery, thousands of Green Lanterns were all looking up at a red-skinned Green Lantern named Sinestro, who stood on a platform above them.

"Abin Sur, the greatest Lantern of all, is gone. He can never be replaced," Sinestro said, looking directly at Hal.

Hal felt the unsure stares of the thousands of Green Lanterns focused on him. He tried to ignore them, but they made him uncomfortable.

"The Guardians have asked for our patience. We must prepare for the battle to come—a great threat to the universe is rising, and we must defeat it. United, we are unstoppable!" Sinestro yelled.

"We are the Green Lantern Corps!" the thousands of Lanterns cheered.

Every Lantern in the hall, except Hal, raised their rings and blasted green energy skyward. Tomar-Re leaned close to Hal.

"Light is a form of energy. It forms a spectrum of color. So, too, there is a spectrum of emotions. Light and emotion are one and the same. We use green because it is the color of *will*," Tomar-Re said. "Will carries out action. It is the ability to create. It gives us our power. Your ring harnesses this power, and it must be recharged at your Lantern battery every twenty-four hours."

Tomar-Re pulled Hal's hand in front of him. "Focus. Your ring can create whatever you think of," Tomar-Re said.

Hal tried to focus on creating something with the ring, but was hit hard from behind and fell to the ground. He pulled himself up to see a giant alien standing above him.

"Never let your guard down, poozer," the giant alien said.

"This is Kilowog. He'll be your combat training officer," Tomar-Re said.

"Welcome to 'Ringslingin' 101,'" Kilowog said.

Kilowog ignited his ring. Two giant, green, glowing fists slammed into Hal.

"I heard about humans. Arrogant, thinking they own the universe," Kilowog said.

Hal tried protecting himself from Kilowog's blows. Finally, he focused and created a shield with his ring.

"You don't gotta be big, you gotta be smart!" Kilowog yelled. "Remember: Your enemy's not gonna play fair!"

That gave Hal an idea. He flew around Kilowog's energy fists until he was directly behind his teacher. He powered up his ring and used its power to propel his body toward Kilowog. With great force, Hal slammed into Kilowog's back with a massive kick.

Kilowog fell hard to the ground. Hal stood proudly over him.

"So, this is the human," a voice said from behind Hal. Hal turned to see Sinestro floating above him.

"I am Sinestro, and you are the human chosen by Abin Sur's ring," Sinestro said, a tone of disgust in his voice. "I'll take it from here, Kilowog."

Hal stood his ground. He could tell Sinestro didn't like him. This was going to be difficult.

Sinestro pointed his ring at Hal and created a green energy sword.

"I smell fear in you," Sinestro sneered. "Fear is the opposite of will. It makes you weak, feeble."

Hal used his ring to re-create his shield, blocking Sinestro's sword. The shield was weak, though, and Sinestro shattered it easily. But Hal refused to give up. He created more weapons from his ring—a spiked club, a battle-ax, and a sledgehammer. Sinestro dodged all of Hal's weapons easily.

Sinestro blasted Hal with green energy weapons, nearly crushing the human.

"You insult Abin Sur's memory by wearing his ring. You are afraid," Sinestro said.

The words hurt Hal because he felt they were true. Sinestro hit Hal with several blasts of green energy.

"When you are afraid, you cannot act. As a Green Lantern, you must fear nothing!" Sinestro screamed.

Sinestro powered up his ring, aiming it at Hal. This was the end.

Hal covered his head, anticipating Sinestro's final blow, but it never came. Sinestro left in disgust. Hal looked up at Tomar-Re and Kilowog, humiliated.

"He's right. I'm only human. Of course we aren't ready to defend the universe," Hal whispered.

"The ring saw something in you; something you don't see in yourself. The ring never makes a mistake," Tomar-Re said.

"This time it did," Hal said sadly as he rocketed toward the atmosphere, going back to Earth.

Hal returned home to his apartment, feeling sorry for himself. He didn't feel worthy of wearing the Green Lantern ring. He felt like a failure. He'd disappointed Carol and Ferris Aircraft, and now he'd let the entire universe down, too. Hal checked his mail and noticed an invitation from Ferris Aircraft. It was inviting Hal to a party at Ferris that night. Surprised at the invitation, Hal decided to go and try to make things better with Carol.

The party was a lavish affair. The rooftop of Ferris Aircraft was decorated beautifully, and the guests were all in a wonderful mood. Carol was wearing a stunning dress and looked prettier to Hal than she ever had. Carol stood next to her father as he approached a microphone.

"We are pleased to announce that despite the accident during the flight demonstration, the government has agreed to purchase the Sabres," Carl announced. Everyone in the party, except Hal, cheered.

Carl Ferris continued speaking, putting his arm around Carol.

"I'm also pleased to announce that my daughter Carol will be taking over for me as the head of Ferris Aircraft!" he announced. Again the guests cheered. This time Hal smiled. He was happy for Carol. She'd always wanted to run Ferris. This was her dream come true.

Carol moved to the microphone to speak, but was interrupted by a terrible noise.

Near the rooftop party, a helicopter had gotten tangled in some cables and was flying out of control. It was on a collision course with a huge electric billboard that stood right above Carol and her father. Everyone at the party was terrified, helpless to stop the impending crash. Everyone except Hal Jordan. Instinctively, Hal slipped the Green Lantern ring onto his finger. The helicopter smashed into the sign, sending both toward the rooftop crowd.

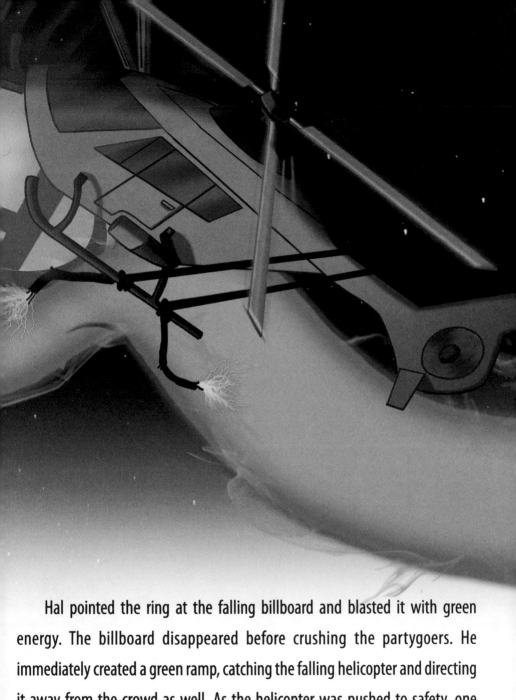

Hal pointed the ring at the falling billboard and blasted it with green energy. The billboard disappeared before crushing the partygoers. He immediately created a green ramp, catching the falling helicopter and directing it away from the crowd as well. As the helicopter was pushed to safety, one of the cables it had snagged whipped around, knocking Carol off the roof. Hal set the helicopter down and dived off the roof after her.

Carol was falling fast. Hal raced down after her. Using the ring, he forced himself to go faster than Carol. He was flying faster than he ever had before. He was getting closer. As Carol approached the ground, Hal shot a stream of green energy from his ring, surrounding her. The green energy slowed Carol's descent and helped pull her close to Hal. He grabbed Carol and held her tightly.

Hal carried Carol through the air and back to the party on the rooftop. The other party guests watched as Hal and Carol, in a green sphere of energy, landed on the rooftop. Carl hurried over to Carol and hugged her. Hal smiled, making eye contact with Carol. She didn't recognize him, but thought there was something familiar about the man who saved her. Hal waved good-bye to the partygoers and flew up into the night sky.

Hal Jordan flew over Coast City. He'd saved Carol without even thinking about it. He'd been wrong. He deserved to be a Green Lantern. The ring that chose him had chosen correctly. As he used the ring, he felt his fear disappear. All that remained was will. He was ready to join the Green Lantern Corps in the great battle that awaited them. In a streak of green, he plowed through the blackness of night, shining brightly the Green Lantern's Light.